A Garland for Gandhi

by Helen Pierce Jacob

illustrated by Lillian Sader

PARNASSUS PRESS BERKELEY, CALIFORNIA

For Lou

Copyright 1968 by Helen Pierce Jacob for story, by Lillian Sader for illustrations
Library of Congress Catalog Card Number 68-21993
Published by Parnassus Press, Berkeley, California
Lithographed in the United States of America

Not so long ago in a country far around the world there lived a girl named Tara. Her village was too small to be noted on the maps of India. Mud huts straggled along the river and dusty footpaths threaded between the huts and the dirt road. Every morning Tara's father went down the river in his boat to fish. When the catch was good, Mother walked to town balancing a full basket on her head. She sold the fish in the market and returned with peas for making dahl, a thick soup, and rice to eat with curry.

Tara had three brothers and a baby sister and, since she was the eldest, she looked after them. When she had scoured the cooking pots with sand, rinsed them in the warm edge of the river, and brought them home, she swung Sita, the baby, to her hip and walked out into the hot Indian sun. Her brothers trailed after her to a place near the river under a giant banyan tree, where they were free to scamper in and out of the water and climb the huge tree in their games.

Uma was Tara's best friend. Often the two met under the wide-spreading tree where they had created their own imaginary house among the tubular hanging roots.

"I wish Sita were my baby sister," Uma said one time.

"Not if you had to take care of her," Tara answered. "She's heavy and squirmy and hot."

"Let me hold her," Uma insisted. Tara gave the baby to her friend, then let her mind wander far away. She began to day-dream. She always dreamed of the same thing — of having some-

thing that was hers alone. Whenever she asked Mother for
something of her own, Mother would smile and say, "Why do
you need this something so much?"

"It would be mine."

"Your bangles are yours."

"Every girl in the village has bangles. I mean something different." Mother would shake her head and turn away and Tara knew she should not ask again.

One day Tara sat on the river bank, Sita asleep on her lap, her brothers splashing in the water. She heard the soft pad of feet in the velvet dust and Uma squatted beside her holding a wriggling furry bundle. Tara stared, then she timidly touched the breathing ball of softness and heard a little whine.

It was a puppy!

"His name is Kala," Uma said. "My uncle came from town last night and brought him to me."

"For your very own?" Tara asked.

"Yes. Uncle said I needed a puppy because I have no brothers or sisters."

"Your very own," Tara said again. She held out her hands and Uma offered the puppy. Tara cuddled him to her neck and felt his silky soft ears. "My uncles bring fish, not puppies," she sighed. Uma laughed and reached for Kala. All morning she played with him and all morning Tara looked on with longing. She could think of nothing she wanted more than a puppy.

It was time for the noon rest and Tara led her brothers back
to the hut where they all stretched out on ragged mats and slept.
But Tara could not sleep; she kept thinking about the puppy. If
only one of her uncles would surprise her as Uma's uncle had
done. But would Father let her keep a pet? . . .

Mother whispered to Tara that it was time for her spinning
lesson. She stepped carefully so she would not wake her baby
sister or her brothers, and followed Mother outside. Sitting
cross-legged on the hard-swept earth before the hut, she watched
Mother unwind enough yarn from the half-filled spindle to
thread through the slots, leaving the loose end on her knee.
Then from a basket she took a sliver, a narrow tube of cotton,

and deftly rolled the end of it until it was thin as yarn. She twisted the new cotton to the end of finished yarn on her knee and slowly, with her other hand, began to turn the wheel that rotated the spindle. Tara watched Mother's skillful fingers stretch the cotton smoothly, as it entered the slots, yet keep the thin strand from breaking. This, for Tara, was the hardest part.

"Father says we spin because of Gandhi. It is strange that such a famous man finds the time to spin. Will I ever see Gandhi?"

"You did once."

"I did?" Tara asked in surprise.

"When you were a baby. Your father and I walked to Baroda to hear Gandhi speak. It took us three days to reach that city."

"And you carried me on your hip as I carry Sita now?"

"Yes."

"Why did you go?"

"Father said I must hear Gandhi."

"Why?"

"Because by his wisdom and work he is a great leader of our people."

"Did Gandhi ask everyone to spin?"

"Yes. He spoke to crowds of people for three nights. He told us that India must be free of the British rule—free to rule itself. He said that spinning and wearing clothes of homespun would help in this struggle."

After Mother had filled the spindle, she gave her place to Tara and watched her daughter begin the threading. Soon Tara started to turn the wheel, but her beginner's fingers could not feed the cotton evenly and the forming yarn parted. Mother put her hand over Tara's small one and helped her hold the yarn evenly. Then she removed her hand and watched her daughter falter on alone. Tara dropped her arms and buried her face in her mother's sari. "I'll never learn," she cried. Mother drew her close.

"Gandhi would be proud to see you spinning."

"But he's far away, and he'll never know that you or I spin or that we wear homespun."

"It isn't important that he sees us," Mother replied. "It is far more important that Uma and her parents and the other villagers see us wearing homespun. It is a sign that we believe in Gandhi's way.''

"Uma laughs at my clothes," Tara complained.

"What do you say when she laughs?"

"What Father has said many times! 'Gandhi is a great man and he will lead us to independence someday — and he wears homespun.' ''

"I hear Sita," Mother said. She got up in one graceful motion and went into the hut.

It was still hot inside the two-room hut as Tara lifted her sister from the woven mat covering the hard dirt floor. Mother had already used a precious match to light the brazier for the evening meal. Tara watched Mother's quick hands over the cooking pot. Did Gandhi know how crowded they were in their small house, or how little rice there was in the corner jar? Would they, and the other families in the village, have more food if India became free, she wondered?

That evening Father came through the narrow doorway followed by his noisy sons. They sat around the brazier as Mother, serving Father first, ladled the food. Father stirred the curry and rice in his round tray, cupped some in his right hand, and pushed the mixture into his mouth with his thumb. Tara, who had been feeding Sita, squeezed into her place in the circle. She daintily tore off a small piece of her chapati, a flat wheat cake, wrapped it around some rice and popped it into her mouth. No one spoke as the family ate. Soon Father leaned back and licked his fingers. This was a sign for Mother to pour water over his hands as she always did when he had finished his meal.

"Father," Tara asked when he was settled again, "how can spinning help fight the British?" He was happy to answer her.

"It is part of swaraj."

"Swaraj?"

"Self-rule. Gandhi urges all Indians, rich or poor, living in cities or villages, no matter how they pray, to work together as brothers; so we will be ready for independence. What we can make for ourselves we should make. If every Indian wears homespun, no one will need to buy British-made cloth. Then the British will know our strength."

"Uma's mother buys the British cloth," Tara said.

"I know," Father said.

"Why doesn't she wear homespun?" Tara asked.

"She does not know of Gandhi's teaching," he said.

"But if she did, she would know he is right! Then maybe Uma could learn to spin!" Tara exclaimed. And looking out through the doorway, there was Uma chasing Kala. Tara squirmed on her mat as Father looked at her and smiled.

"May I go out now, Father?"

When he nodded yes, Tara jumped up and ran to Uma. The two friends and the little dog danced and laughed and yelped all around the yard until it was dark.

As she went to her bed that night Tara asked if she could have a puppy.

"No," Father said without looking at her.

"Uma has one."

"I know. Who gave it to her?"

"Her uncle."

"Her father owns three boats and he has only one child to feed," Father said. "I have one boat and seven mouths to feed."

"A puppy doesn't eat much," Tara said softly.

"He will grow up."

"He can share my food," she said desperately.

"No, you have little enough," Father said. "Go to sleep."

Two days later Uma let Tara take Kala home during the noon rest. The puppy slept on Tara's mat and when she got up to spin he woke and bounced after her, tail erect. He put his nose against the spinning wheel and sniffed it all over, then backed off and barked as she began to turn the wheel. When he scampered away, Tara had to get up and bring him back. She held him in the curve of her shoulder. "If only you were mine," she whispered. That day she filled but half a spindle and Mother frowned. Tara was almost finished with her first tikla of yarn and Mother was anxious to have it done. It seemed to Tara that she would never finish that certain length of thread to complete her tikla.

In the evening fishermen sat cross-legged on the packed earth, or rested on charpoys, the low cots on their verandas. They talked of the day's fishing while their wives gossiped and children shouted along the river. Smoke from the evening fires hung in the air and the leaves of the banyan tree were mirrored in the still water. The stifling heat lingered long after sundown.

One evening a stranger came along the path by the river and asked for the headman. The curious villagers drifted toward him. The stranger was dressed in coarse clothing and wore a narrow white hat slanted over his forehead. "He is a Gandhi man," Father said, pointing to his clothes. "See, he wears homespun like ours." Mother nodded and Tara looked at the stranger with new interest. She had never seen anyone dressed in homespun except her own family.

Krishna Das, the headman of the village, came to meet the stranger and together they walked to the banyan tree near the river. The people of the village waited a short distance away. At last, as the fiery sun slipped below the horizon, Krishna Das called for everyone to come closer. Tara edged for a place where she could see the stranger. "Why is he here?" she asked. "Be quiet," Mother whispered, "and listen."

"This man is named Jagin Patel. He comes from distant Ahmedabad with important news. I will let him tell you, himself." Jagin Patel stood up slowly, his bronzed arms raised in greeting. Tara could see his worn sandals and the dust covering his vest and trousers.

"My native village is Matwab," he began, "where my father was headman. One day the British police arrested my father because he had urged his people not to buy British-made cloth. If all Indians wore homespun instead of British cloth, he believed, there would be more work and food for Indians. A few days after his arrest, my father was sentenced by a British judge and taken to prison. I never saw him again, alive. He fell sick two months later and died."

An angry groan arose from the circle of villagers. Tara looked toward Father. His face was like stone.

Jagin Patel spoke again: "In grief, I moved with my family to Ahmedabad. It was hard to shake my despair and anger over my father's death. He was a good man; why should he die in prison when he had done nothing wrong? I knew then how cruel and unjust some British laws are, and made a vow to work for India's freedom, even at the risk of my life."

Tara's father spoke out: "Good, good."

"At first, I thought I should take up arms and join with others who believed as I did. Then I heard that Mahatma Gandhi lived nearby in his ashram. In this secluded group of huts and

gardens Gandhi worked and lived peacefully with his family and loyal friends. I wondered, could a man who lived no better than you or I lead India to independence? Gandhi called a meeting and thousands came, many walking tens of miles. I went with my friends and stood close to Gandhi. His height is about the same as mine, his body thin for he eats little, his face round and wrinkled and smiling. His rough homespun and plain sandals gave no hint of his greatness. When he spoke his words were plain, so even those among us who never went to school could understand. He spoke of the people of India, how children go without food because their fathers cannot find work or are not able to grow crops in the barren soil. He reminded us that we live fewer years than people in many other lands because we do not have enough doctors and medicine and hospitals. Indian families would have better houses, more schools and books and roads, if we could work together by self-rule. Most of all, Gandhi told the throng all around him: 'Every Indian must be free to say and to write what he thinks without fear of British laws.' "

Tara's father was one of many listeners to spring up and shout, "Yes! This is true! True!" It was minutes before Krishna Das could quiet the villagers.

"Then Gandhi told us what we must do to win our freedom. We must resist British rule; we must not buy British-made goods. Should force and guns be used against us, *we* will not use force or guns. We will fight with all our strength but our resistance will be peaceful. The British soldiers and police may arrest our people, beat them, even kill them, but we will not beat or kill in return. The world has known too many battles and too much blood, and people still suffer. We will win our freedom by this new way, the way of peace. Our numbers are so great that in time the British will see they cannot force us to violence. Then they will leave India and we will rule ourselves.

"The meeting was over. I walked home with my friends, Gandhi's words singing in my head. Could I be at peace with my enemies? . . . the police and the judge who sent my father to prison to die? Would they leave India because we fight them as Gandhi tells us? I argued with my friends that night and the days that followed. And now I see Gandhi's way is true, and I work with him for our independence. I live at the ashram, learn from him, and teach others."

Jagin Patel paused. "Shall I tell you more?" he asked his audience. Tara could hear Uma's high voice call with the others, "Yes! More, more!" He lifted his hand and spoke:

"Gandhi would not ask us to do anything he has not done himself. He has broken British laws and spent many months in prison. And he has gone without food. He has fasted until he was so weak we feared he would die. Indian men have closed their shops, put down their tools, left their fields, because they believed in Gandhi, and many were beaten and arrested. But freedom has not come. When Gandhi last returned to his ashram from prison, he was not sure of what to do next. He talked with other Indian leaders. He spent many days and weeks in prayer, in silence, and in thought. And now he has decided what must be done. It is this." Patel paused and the villagers listened.

"He will break the Salt Laws!" A babble rose up from the listeners. "For too long Indians have paid a tax to the British on salt; salt, a gift of nature which we need to keep alive. Even the poorest among us have to pay this tax. If tens upon tens of

thousands break the Salt Laws, as Gandhi does, then the British would know that we will disobey other unjust laws as well. It could bring us closer to independence.

"Nineteen days ago Gandhi left his ashram and began his walk to the sea — to Dandi. At the shore he will pick up salt and use it, a sign that he has broken the law. From every village along the way, people leave their homes and walk with Gandhi. The line of marchers grows very long. I come ahead, to tell you that he will pass through your village in four days. How will you greet him?" Patel wiped his wet face and sat down.

"He has told his story well! Now everyone will understand," Father whispered.

Das, the headman, stood. "Our village is honored," he spoke with dignity. "We will greet Gandhi and his marchers when they come. Tomorrow Jagin Patel will meet with us again to talk about the welcome."

Returning home with her mother and father, Tara held her

slim body straight, with her head tilted high, conscious of all the eyes that followed her family. Villagers clustered around Father; one of their own was a Gandhi man.

The next day, as Tara sat at her spinning, Uma came to watch. "Is it hard?" she asked.

"Yes," Tara answered.

"May I try?" Uma said. She tried to imitate Tara's hands at the wheel. In a few minutes she dropped the snarled yarn. "It is hard," she said. "I would rather play with Kala."

"I would rather play with Kala, too," Tara thought. But today she was glad she was learning to spin.

After the evening rice had been eaten, the people of the village waited for Jagin Patel. His figure soon appeared striding down the dusty path. He stopped to greet Father and the two men walked to the banyan tree and sat with Das. Tara's dark eyes and long braid shone as she sat with Mother among the women.

Patel smiled at the gathering of people. His voice was strong

as he continued his talk of the night before. "Gandhi walks ten miles each day, every night resting in another village. The people welcome him with music and waving flags. They build arches and offer him flowers as he enters, and paths are sprinkled with water and fresh tulsi leaves to cool his feet. Soon after Gandhi leaves your village he will reach the sea. There he will pick up the forbidden salt. With him thousands of Indians will take salt along the coast and not pay the tax."

As Patel paused to drink a cup of water, Tara looked around her. It seemed that every neighbor and villager was at the meeting. "This has not happened before," she thought. "Gandhi does bring our people together."

Again Patel spoke. "Gandhi is a great leader because he loves all people and never rests in his fight to free India of British rule. What can you do, here in your village, for freedom? Gandhi believes that spinning and weaving and the wearing of homespun by all Indians will help us win self-rule. Not guns or fighting, but quiet work at the spinning wheel will bring victory. Every day Gandhi spins his length of yarn. I do the same." Then Patel took Father by the arm, asking him to stand. "This man and his wife spin. They are working for freedom, for swaraj." The crowd cheered its approval of Father and he saw Mother and Tara smiling up at him.

Then the people settled back to listen to Das. He began by saying that he and Patel had formed a plan to welcome Gandhi.

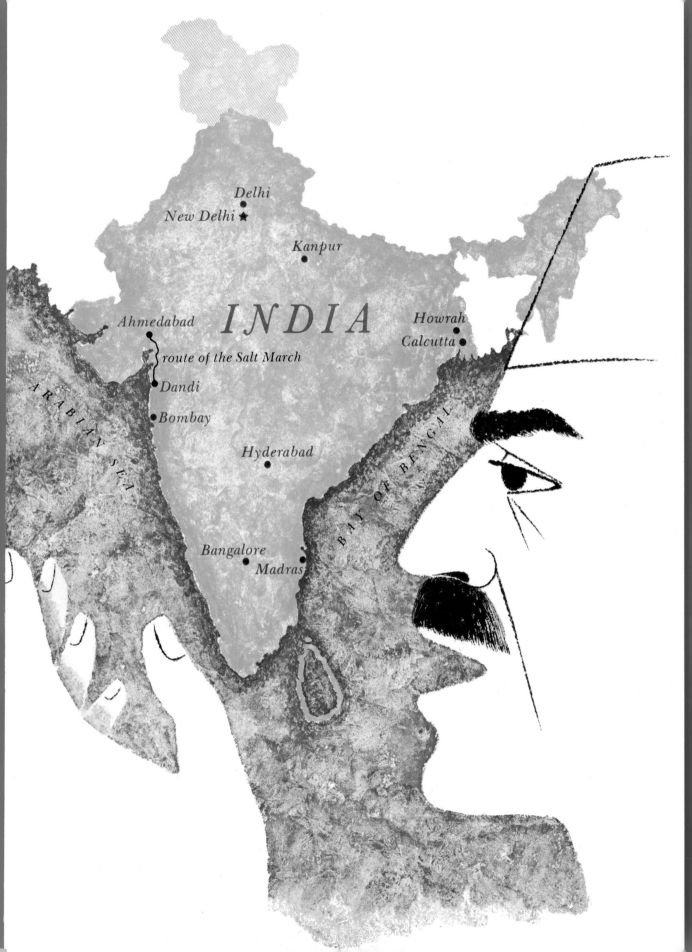

An archway would be built, food and water would be provided, as well as a resting place for Gandhi's overnight stay. Every family was given a task so that all could share in the welcome. Tara's father received the high honor of preparing the welcoming garland. The meeting ended in a buzz of excitement.

For Tara the time passed slowly, then suddenly it was the day of Gandhi's arrival. He was expected to reach their village late

in the afternoon. Father edged his boat along the river through the shallow marshy spots where he found brilliant, dewy flowers. Mother met him during the noon rest with a large basket and carefully they unloaded the fragile blossoms. Through the long, hot afternoon they worked with the gold and silver thread that Mother had brought from the market. When the sun's rays slanted lower in the sky, the garland was finished. Tara looked

at the thick circle of white and golden flowers held by strings of gold and silver woven in a simple design. She had never seen anything so lovely, and she ran to tell Uma. The two girls came back to the hut, Uma carrying her puppy, and they stood admiring the garland.

A young boy pushed into the crowded room calling for Father. "Krishna Das would like to see you . . . right now," he sputtered. And as Father hurried away toward the house of the headman, Mother took the bucket and went to draw water from the well for baths, her sons tagging along after her. Tara, Uma and the playful Kala stayed with the baby.

Both girls heard shouts coming from the road. Could it be Gandhi arriving early? They ran outside and along the path, and saw that it was only two excited boys helping their father put the final touches on the welcoming arch. When Tara and Uma returned to the hut they stopped in horror at what they saw.

Kala was pawing and chewing the magnificent garland!

Uma grabbed the little dog and pulled him away. Tara let out a sharp cry but she couldn't move. Suddenly everyone was in the hut and Uma, in tears, ran home with her puppy. Father fingered the ruined garland with trembling hands, Mother hovering beside him. "Gandhi will be here soon and there is no garland." His shoulders bent over the broken flowers and chewed threads. "Go!" he pushed Tara roughly. "Take your

brothers and sister and don't come until I call you!"

Tara swept her brothers ahead of her and stumbled toward the river. She sat in her private house among the banyan roots, and, burying her face in her baby sister's smooth neck, she cried. How had it happened? Why hadn't Uma taken the puppy with her when they left the hut? Her brothers stood frightened, watching her body shake with sobs.

The sun, almost touching the horizon, told Tara it was time for Gandhi's arrival. She saw the first eager villagers hastening toward the welcome arch. She waited. More villagers were leaving their huts as she stood up and shaded her eyes. Surely Father would call soon. Was he so angry that he would not let her go to the ceremonies? She could hear the rapid talk and laughter of people gathering around the arch. Then she heard a voice cry out.

"Gandhiji ki jai!"

Many voices rose up as one — "Long live Gandhi!" Tara ran a few steps. Where were Father and Mother? Had they made a new garland? What would Das do if there was no welcoming garland?

Now Father called. Tara shouted to her brothers and ran up the lane after her parents. Mother and Father carried something

between them that she could not see; it was covered with a cloth.

"Gandhiji ki jai!" chanted the villagers. "Gandhiji ki jai!" Tara saw a long line of marchers trailing far off to a bend in the road. The first marcher was a small man bearing down on a walking stick. It was Gandhi! He came closer and closer. Tara felt a shiver of excitement. *This is the man of peace who is leading India to freedom. This is the man my father and mother love and for whom we spin and wear homespun.*

Gandhi's stride was long and firm as he entered the shade of the welcoming arch. Tara could see his dusty eyeglasses and the wrinkles in his face. He stood before Krishna Das and they exchanged cordial greetings. It was time for the garland! Das turned to Father who quietly removed the cloth covering from the object he held. The headman gasped and the crowd of villagers grew still.

The welcoming garland was Tara's first imperfect tikla of homespun yarn with one bright flower hanging from it!

Das hesitated, his face frozen in utter surprise. But before he could speak, Gandhi touched his arm, and with dignity bowed his head, so that the headman could place the slim garland around his neck. Gandhi ran his fingers over the knot-filled strands of yarn. Then he smiled and spoke to the hushed people.

"I see there is a spinner among you who has given her tikla to welcome me. Who is she?" He held out a thin brown arm, waiting. Tara heard him, but her legs would not move. Mother pushed her forward, toward Gandhi. He came over to her, bent down, and asked, "Is it your first tikla?"

"Yes."

He laughed a delighted laugh and putting his hand on Tara's shoulder, turned her to face the villagers. Then, so all could hear, he said:

"Many, many years ago, our people made their own cloth. Every mother in India did this work. My own mother used to spin yarn and wear coarse cloth, though she had the money to buy finer cloth. She did it because she loved our old ways and found joy in spinning. Every man, woman and child should learn to spin. Then they will no longer look to the British for cloth. More than anything I can do, it will be a sign to the British rulers that the people of India are united and their independence must come soon.

"I am marching to the sea, a short journey from your village. There I shall break the Salt Laws. Many, many others will do the same. Salt, like air and water, is needed for life; and it is needed even more by the sweating poor man working under the hot sun of India. That is truth. The British know my plan and their police will be ready to arrest me and those with me. We will submit without fighting or turmoil. It is the only way to freedom. In the end our way will have greater strength than bullets and swords.

"This tikla is a symbol of that way. Bless this spinner. I shall always remember her gift and your village."

Tara stood looking up into Gandhi's smiling face. She had made a garland for Gandhi.

HISTORICAL NOTE

The part of this story which tells of Mahatma Gandhi's "march" to the sea to break the Salt Laws is based on history. In 1928 and 1929, because the British government would not grant India independence, Gandhi and millions of Indian people refused to abide by certain laws. Under Gandhi's leadership actions were taken against British rule, actions without violence. It was Gandhi's dream for India to win independence without war. These actions of "non-violence" and "civil disobedience" were India's only hope, he said.

At the end of 1929, with growing oppression and unrest, Gandhi feared a bloody clash. After weeks of silent thought he decided that to avoid violence, but to show the British government and the world India's will for independence, he would lead in the act of breaking the Salt Laws. Salt was highly priced and taxed and he reasoned that such a basic need should cost very little. Gandhi decided to journey on foot with a group of 78 followers from his ashram in Ahmedabad, for 200 miles to Dandi on the Arabian Sea. The "Salt March" began on March 12, 1930, and on the morning of April 5th, Gandhi reached the shore and picked up the forbidden salt. Thousands with him and in other parts of India did the same. A month later Gandhi was arrested and sent to prison. By the next year the Salt Laws were changed for the better; but more important, the response of the Indian people to the Salt March made clear that the time of British rule was coming to an end.

Peaceful, non-violent resistance continued for many years until independence was won on August 15, 1947. In January 1948, Mahatma Gandhi died by assassination after having devoted a lifetime to uplifting his people of India.

Mohandas K. Gandhi was born October 1869, and died January 1948. The name "Mahatma" was given to him, it is said, by the Indian poet Tagore and means "The Great Soul."

As this book neared completion, the world mourned the assassination of Martin Luther King, Jr., Nobel Peace Prize winner in 1964 and eminent civil rights leader, whose doctrine of non-violence resembled so closely the teaching of Mahatma Gandhi. We learned also that the illustrator drew inspiration, in her work, from a deep admiration for both Mahatma Gandhi and Martin Luther King, Jr.

GLOSSARY

ashram	A secluded settlement of people with similar beliefs who work, live, teach and learn together.
bangles	Brightly colored rings worn as bracelets or anklets, usually several together.
chapati	A flat pancake made of wheat flour.
charpoy	A portable wooden cot with rope lacings.
curry	A highly spiced Indian dish made with vegetables or meat, cooked with curry seasoning.
dahl	A very thick pea soup.
Gandhi*ji*	Term of love or respect.
Gandhiji ki jai	Long life to Gandhi or Victory for Gandhi.
sari	A woman's garment: yards of cloth wrapped and draped around the body, one end forming a skirt, the other end a shoulder or head covering.
swaraj	Swa—self; raj—rule. Self rule or independence.
tikla	640 threads of homespun wound in a circle, the length of one's arm.

The map in this book is of present-day India.